THE LIGHTNING ESCAPE

And
OTHER STORIES

The Fairfield Friends Devotional Adventures

Firecracker Power and Other Stories
The Lightning Escape and Other Stories

9702

NANCY SPECK

A FAIRFIELD FRIENDS DEVOTIONAL ADVENTURE

THE LIGHTNING ESCAPE
And OTHER STORIES

BETHANY HOUSE PUBLISHERS
MINNEAPOLIS, MINNESOTA 55438

The Lightning Escape and Other Stories
Copyright © 1997
Nancy Speck

Cover illustration by Neverne Covington
Story illustrations by Joe Nordstrom

Published by Bethany House Publishers
A Ministry of Bethany Fellowship, Inc.
11300 Hampshire Avenue South
Minneapolis, Minnesota 55438

Printed in the United States of America.

Library of Congress Cataloging-in-Publication Data

Speck, Nancy
    The lightning escape and other stories with take-away value / Nancy Speck.
         p. cm. — (A Fairfield Friends devotional adventure)
    Summary: The Fairfield Friends make discoveries about honesty, generosity, and following the word of the Lord. Each episode is followed by questions and suggested Bible verses.
    ISBN 1-55661-962-6 (pbk.)
    [1. Christian life—Fiction.] I. Title. II. Series: Speck, Nancy. Fairfield friends devotional adventure.
    PZ7.S7412Li 1996
    [Fic]—dc21   97-4651
                                                     CIP
                                                    AC

To Brian

Thanks for Cameron . . .

and everything else.

NANCY SPECK is a free-lance writer and home-maker who has published numerous articles, stories, and poems. Her background in creative writing and social work gives her unique insight into the importance and challenge of teaching children Christian character traits at an early age. Nancy and her husband, Brian, have two elementary-age daughters and make their home in Pennsylvania.

Contents

Cameron Parker

Cameron is very smart in math and science and is in third grade at a private school, Foster Academy. He lives with his parents, older brother, Philip, and younger sister, Justine.

Ceely Coleman

Ceely, short for Cecilia, is hardworking and serious. She is in fourth grade at Morgandale Christian School, plays field hockey, and has a black cat named Snowball.

Hutch Coleman

Hutch, short for Hutchinson, is Ceely's younger brother. He's a second grader at Morgandale Christian School and is the class clown.

Min Hing

Min, a third-grade student at Fairfield Elementary, lives with her parents and grandmother. She's quiet and shy, takes ballet lessons, and plays the piano.

Valerie Stevens

Valerie lives with her mother and little sister, Bonnie, since her parents are divorced. Valerie, who is friendly and outspoken, is an average student in second grade at Fairfield Elementary.

Roberto Ruiz

Roberto, a fourth grader at Fairfield Elementary, has lived with his grandpop ever since his parents died. His older brother, Ramone, lives with them. Roberto plays soccer and has a dog named Freckles.

1

The World of Billy Bongo

Good morning, Mr. and Mrs. Hing, Grand-mother Hing."

The Hing family smiled at Pastor Tran as he shook their hands on their way out of the church.

He turned to Min. "Everything is set for your project next Saturday. How about if I meet you and your friends here around 9:00?"

"That sounds great," said Min. "Thank you."

As the Hing family walked to their car, Min thought about her service project. She hoped it would help her win the camp scholarship. Her church gave it every two years to a third or fourth grader who showed good Christian character.

Min had decided to fix up the flower beds

around the church. Her friends in the Fairfield Court neighborhood had agreed to help her. When Min got home, she phoned Ceely and Hutch, Cameron, Roberto, and Valerie and told them the details.

The next day, Min walked to ballet class after school. As she entered the dance studio, she stopped and stared. Half the girls had on T-shirts with a weird cartoon character on it. Underneath the picture it said "Billy Bongo."

"Hi, Min. Like my shirt?" Ashley questioned, running up to her.

"Who's Billy Bongo?" asked Min.

The other girls stopped what they were doing and looked at Min, their mouths hanging open in surprise.

"You mean you haven't seen the new Billy Bongo cartoon?" asked Ashley. "It started several weeks ago. It's on every night at 7:00."

I do my devotions every night at that time, thought Min. "What's so great about him?" she asked.

"He does all this really cool stuff," Ashley answered. "You should watch it, Min."

That evening, after Min finished her homework, she opened her Bible and devotion book. She glanced at the clock. It was 7:00. Min tried to read her Bible, but she couldn't keep her mind on it. Finally she closed the Bible and turned on the small TV in her room. She kept the volume down low. After closing her door, she clicked on channel 42 and began to watch the Billy Bongo show.

At first Min didn't like Billy Bongo. *He doesn't respect his parents or teachers,* thought Min. *He doesn't do his homework.* "Oh, gross!" Min exclaimed out loud. Billy had shoved two green beans up his nose. *But he is funny when he talks in that silly voice,* Min decided. *And the other kids always hang around him and do what he does.* By the third night, Min was hooked.

Each day at the ballet studio, Min and the others pretended to be Billy Bongo. They walked and talked like him and did the things he did on the show. More and more of them showed up in Billy Bongo T-shirts. Min really wanted a shirt, too.

I've saved a lot of my allowance for a case for my Bible, thought Min during ballet class. *I could use the money for a shirt. But Mother and Father would never allow me to buy one. Maybe I can work something out, though.*

"Mother, could I stop at the mall after my piano lesson?" Min asked the next day. "I almost have enough money saved for my Bible case. I want to stop by the Hosanna Christian

Book Store and look at the different kinds they have.''

"I guess you can go," said her mother. "But you still have to finish your homework and do your devotions.''

"I know. Thanks, Mother.''

After her lesson, Min hurried to the mall. She walked past the drug store, the Hosanna Christian Book Store, and into the Y-Mart. Ten minutes later, Min strolled out of the store with a Billy Bongo T-shirt she had just bought. She stopped at the bathroom, put the shirt on under her sweat shirt, and threw the bag in the trash can.

———

That Saturday, Min again wore the T-shirt under her sweat shirt. After her father dropped her off at the church, she unzipped her sweat shirt and waited for her friends to arrive.

Ceely and Hutch arrived first. "What's on your T-shirt?" asked Ceely.

"It's Billy Bongo," said Min proudly.

"Who's that?" Hutch questioned. "I've never even heard of him.''

While Min explained Billy and the TV show, Roberto, Valerie, and Cameron arrived.

"Min, why are you wearing one of those

silly T-shirts?" said Roberto when he saw the shirt.

"Do you guys know about Billy Bongo?" asked Ceely.

"Yeah," answered Valerie. "A whole bunch of kids wear the shirts at school. My mom won't let me watch the show, though."

"My parents won't either," Cameron said.

"My grandpop says it's not a good show for kids," said Roberto.

"We'd never be able to wear shirts like that at the Christian school," said Hutch.

"OK, OK," said Min. "So you don't like him. I think he's funny, and so do lots of kids."

Suddenly a truck turned into the parking lot. "Hi, everyone," called Pastor Tran, waving out the window.

The friends met up with him in back of the church. Pastor Tran showed them the flower beds that needed to be cleared of dead weeds and brush. He got out shovels so they could remove rocks.

"You're in charge, Min, since this is your project. I'll be in my office"—he stopped when he saw what was on Min's T-shirt—"doing some work if you need me," he finished. He turned and walked toward the church but glanced back at Min twice, frowning both times.

As they worked, Min acted goofy and silly like Billy Bongo. One time Min looked up and saw Pastor Tran watching her through the window. She waved to him excitedly. He barely raised his arm to wave back.

The following Thursday, Min and two others met at the church to find out who won the camp scholarship. Min read her essay on Christian character in front of the judges and told about her service project. An interview with them followed. Finally, she and the others

waited in a Sunday school room for the judges' decision. The judges were Pastor Tran, two men from the board of elders, and two Sunday school teachers.

After twenty minutes, they returned. As the winner's name was announced, tears formed in Min's eyes. But they were sad tears, not happy ones. Min had lost.

As she began to leave the church, Pastor Tran called her into his office. "Min, I'm very sorry you didn't win the scholarship. I know how much you wanted to go." He paused. "You know, you were the favorite to win the scholarship until this past Saturday."

Min looked at him, puzzled.

"When I saw your Billy Bongo shirt and the way you tried to act like him, I was very surprised and disappointed. I saw a big change in you. First John 2:15 says, 'Do not love the world or the things in the world. If anyone loves the world, the love of the father is not in him.'" He waited while the verses sank in. "The other judges and I felt we had to award the scholarship to someone else."

Min nodded silently and left the church. When her father picked her up, she told him she hadn't won. At home, Min went straight to her room. She didn't even want any supper.

At 7:00 she turned on Billy Bongo. But he didn't seem very funny anymore. Min turned off the TV and stuffed her Billy Bongo shirt in the bottom of her drawer. Then she opened her Bible and began her devotions.

The Lightning Escape

Things to Think About

Why did Min start to watch the Billy Bongo show?

_____

_____

How did Min change after watching it?

_____

_____

Why did Min stop watching the Billy Bongo show?

_____

_____

Read Matthew 16:26 and 1 Corinthians 3:19a. What happens if you follow the world or seek after the things in the world?

_____

_____

Read Romans 12:2 and 1 John 5:4–5. How can you overcome the world and its power?

_____

_____

Read James 2:5 and 1 John 2:15–17. What good things happen when you turn away from what the world wants you to have?

_____

_____

Let's Act It Out!

Memorize 1 John 2:15.

Make a list of things that worldly or non-Christian people think are important.

_____

_____

_____

_____

Make a list of items that Christians think are important.

_____

_____

_____

_____

The Lightning Escape

Talk about things you can do to fight off worldly traps.

List the TV programs you watch. What are the good things about each of the shows? What are the bad things about each one? Decide whether you should keep watching each show.

_____

_____

_____

_____

_____

_____

2

Straws, a Notebook, and a Bike

Rats," said Hutch as the school bell rang. He hadn't finished his art project. While his classmates put away books and got ready to leave, Hutch put away his supplies in the art corner. Then he picked up three pieces of construction paper and several markers. *I can work on my project at home,* he thought.

In the school yard, Hutch waved to Ceely as she got on their bus. But Hutch continued on to the bike racks. He grinned as he saw the new red-and-silver Trailhead bike he'd just gotten for his birthday.

Hutch strapped on his helmet and hopped onto his bike. After doing wheelies across the playground, he turned onto Conway Street. He cut up the alley behind Walnut and turned into the library parking lot. Inside, he told a librarian he needed some bug books for a school report. Hutch followed her to the card catalog.

"Here we go," she said, pulling out a drawer. "These are all the books we have on bugs." She handed him a piece of paper and a pencil. "Copy down the titles you want to look up. This is the reference number. You'll find these on shelf ten and the ones with this number on shelf four." She pointed to each shelf across the room.

Hutch copied three book names and their numbers and hurried to shelf ten. On the way, he shoved the pencil in his pants pocket.

After riding home, Hutch carefully parked his bike in the garage. "Where's Mom?" Hutch asked Ceely when he got inside. He wanted to show her his books.

"Upstairs changing clothes," answered Ceely. "She has a church meeting tonight that she had forgotten about, so we're eating at Uncle Elmo's Burger Barn."

"Yes!" shouted Hutch. Uncle Elmo's was his favorite fast food burger restaurant.

After they met their dad there, they

ordered. "I want an Uncle Elmo Burger, fries, and a chocolate milk shake," Hutch said, smacking his lips. Then he saw the new straws. They had colored stripes twirling around them. "Awesome," he said. He nudged Ceely. "Look at the straws."

"Cool," said Ceely. They each took one for their drinks.

When it was time to go, Hutch emptied the trash and returned the tray. On the way back, he got six more straws. He stuck them in his jacket pocket. *The guys at school will love these.*

The next day, when Hutch parked his bike, he saw a notebook lying on the ground. *Wow,* he thought, flipping through the pages. *It's practically new.* When he closed it, he saw E.J. written on the front. Hutch shrugged. *I have no idea who E.J. is.* He stuck the notebook in his pack and hurried into school.

At lunch, Hutch passed out the straws to his buddies. During the afternoon, he used the library pencil and some notebook paper from the one he'd found. And at art class, he discovered he'd forgotten to bring back the markers.

After school, Hutch ran out the side door to the playground. He rounded the corner of the building and froze in his steps. "Where's my bike?'' he asked out loud.

Hutch looked around frantically. No one was riding it, and it hadn't been moved to another rack. He asked some other kids on the playground, but no one had seen it. Finally, Hutch trudged back into the school to call his mom.

"Hutch, what are you doing here?"

Hutch turned. It was Mrs. Martin, his teacher. "Somebody stole my new bike," answered Hutch, his voice shaking.

"Oh, Hutch. I'm so sorry. Can I give you a ride home?"

Hutch nodded silently.

————

The next day, Mrs. Martin told her students about Hutch's stolen bike. "Did anyone see anyone around the bike racks yesterday?" she asked. But no one had.

"Stealing is a serious matter," she continued. "Some stealing is obvious, like with Hutch's bike. But there are other kinds of stealing as well."

Hutch frowned. *What other kinds of stealing could there be?* he wondered.

"Suppose a family takes home some towels from the motel they're staying in while on vacation. That's stealing." Mrs. Martin picked up her Bible from her desk. "Another example is found in Leviticus 6:3. 'He might find something that had been lost. . . .' If he keeps what he found without trying to find the owner," added Mrs. Martin, "that's a form of stealing."

Hutch sat up in his chair. *The notebook,* he thought.

"Or what if employees in an office take paper, pens, or paper clips to use at home?" Mrs. Martin suggested. "Or maybe they 'borrow' a stapler and keep forgetting to return it? All of these are examples of stealing.''

The straws, thought Hutch, *and the library pencil and the art supplies*. He studied the wood grain in his desk. *I never thought I was* . . . Hutch couldn't even say the word in his head.

Mrs. Martin continued. ''Leviticus 6:4 tells us what someone must do if he's stolen something. 'He must bring back whatever he stole.' ''

Hutch knew what he had to do. Over the next several days, he returned the paper and markers and the pencil. He turned in the notebook at the school office. The secretary easily found Ellen Jenkins, E.J., in the school roster. Finally, after telling his parents about everything, including the straws, they drove him to Uncle Elmo's. Hutch turned over 30 cents of his allowance to the manager, the cost of the six straws he took.

I know I made things right, thought Hutch while feeding his lizards and fish in his room. *I just wish someone would make it right with me by returning my bike. I wish I could tell the person the Bible verses, but how do I do that?*

Hutch continued to think while he cleaned out his turtle cage. ''The comment line,'' he said out loud. ''That's it!''

The Lightning Escape

Hutch searched through yesterday's *Morgandale Daily Sentinel*. His parents always talked about the comments that people called in to the newspaper. After finding the number, he raced to the phone.

———

Three days later, his comment appeared. Hutch read it softly. " 'Whoever stole the new red and silver Trailhead bike from the Morgandale Christian School, please return it. In Leviticus 6:4 it says you are to return what you stole.' " Hutch didn't know if the person would read it, care about the Bible verse, or return it. But it was worth a try.

Every day after that, Hutch checked the bike rack. Nothing. After two weeks, ready to give up, he almost didn't bother to check. But he couldn't help himself. *Maybe . . . just maybe,* thought Hutch as he turned the corner. And there it was, parked in the rack, dirty but in good shape. Hutch rode home as fast as he could to show his mom and Ceely.

After finishing his homework, he washed and shined his bike up as good as new. He was just putting away the bucket when his dad came home.

"Looks like what you said in the newspaper

got to someone after all," said his dad. He patted Hutch on the back.

A little later, Dad called Hutch into the living room. "Look what I found in the paper," he said. Hutch sat down next to him, and Dad pointed to a message printed in the comment section.

Hutch read it out loud. " 'To the owner of the red-and-silver bike: Thanks for the Bible verse. Sorry.' "

"Yes!" exclaimed Hutch. He ran outside and jumped on his bike. Then he rode happily around the block, doing wheelies all the way.

The Lightning Escape
Things to Think About

What things had Hutch taken that didn't
belong to him?

_____

_____

What did Hutch learn from his teacher and
the Bible about stealing?

_____

_____

Why do you think Hutch's bike was returned?

_____

_____

Read Genesis 27:1–38. What did Jacob steal
from Esau? Why?

_____

_____

Read Exodus 20:15. What is this verse a part
of? Why do you think God added stealing?

_____

_____

A Fairfield Friends Devotional Adventure

Let's Act It Out!

Memorize Exodus 20:15.

Using Leviticus 6:2–4, think of and write down different examples of stealing. Then talk about them.

_____

_____

Think of an item that is very important to you. Tell or draw a picture of how you would feel if it was stolen.

3

Cheating God

Mom! Mom!" yelled Valerie as she charged through the front door. "You know that craft kit I showed you that can be used to make all kinds of stuff?"

"I remember it, and I also remember telling you I couldn't afford to buy it," answered Mom.

"But I can buy it myself now," Valerie said. "Mrs. Long down the street broke her leg, and she asked me to walk her dog after school. She said she'd pay me a dollar a day. Can I do it?"

Valerie's mom thought a moment and then smiled. "I suppose you can, but 50 cents of the money must be put in the offering plate each week."

Valerie's mouth dropped open as she stared at her mom. She couldn't speak.

Mom sighed. "It says in the Bible, Numbers 18:26, I think, that a tenth of your money should be given back to God."

"That's not fair," Valerie said angrily. "It'll take me a whole lot longer to save for the craft kit."

"Well, that may be, but you *will* give 50 cents to God on Sunday," answered Mom firmly. She added her look that meant, *I've made a decision and we're done talking about it.*

Valerie grabbed her backpack and stomped to her bedroom. She flung herself onto her bed. *It's just not fair*, she thought. *I do all the work, then have to give up some of my earnings. There must be a way I can keep it.* Valerie stared at the ceiling, her forehead wrinkled. Suddenly she smiled. *I've got it!*

That Sunday, Valerie sat in church with her mom. Her little sister, Bonnie, sat on her mom's lap. It was almost time for the offering. Valerie glanced at her mom, who was watching her. After pulling two silver coins out of her wallet, she held them in her hand.

The usher passed the offering plate to Valerie's mom, who put in a check. Then she passed it to Valerie. Valerie's two nickels clinked the side as she put them in.

Valerie smiled. *I got away with it! I'll get the*

craft kit sooner now, and . . . well . . . I still gave 10 cents to God.

During the next week, Valerie walked Colby, Mrs. Long's dog, every day. She watched her dollars and change grow. When she had enough, she cut out the order blank. Then she sneaked an envelope and stamp from the kitchen drawer. *I sure can't let Mom know I'm doing this*, thought Valerie. *She knows I shouldn't have enough saved yet.*

After Valerie filled in her name and address, she counted out the exact amount she needed. She added the extra 50 cents for postage, too. Finally, she put it all into the envelope. The loose coins jingled inside. While her mom put Bonnie down for a nap, Valerie ran to the corner mailbox and slid the envelope into the slot.

The magazine ad said the kit would arrive in seven to ten days. Valerie always got the mail on her way in from school. She knew she'd have no problem getting the kit to her room without her mom seeing it.

But on the seventh day, no craft kit was delivered. After ten days, it still hadn't arrived. Valerie checked the mail for several days after that, but still no kit.

———

"Why the long face?" asked Mom as she walked into the living room a few days later.

"Oh . . . nothing," Valerie answered, shrugging as she stared sadly out the window.

"I know," said Mom. "Let's count up your money and fill out the order blank for your craft kit. I'm sure you have more than enough by now."

Tears formed in Valerie's eyes. "Oh, Mom," she cried, "I only put 10 cents in the offering plate and kept the rest. I already sent my money in, but the kit never came. I know what I did was wrong. I'm really sorry."

Without a word, Mom picked up her Bible off the end table. She turned to the middle of the Bible. "Proverbs 11:24," she began. " 'Some people give much but get back even more. But others don't give what they should, and they end up poor.' "

Mom stood up. "You think about that while I make a phone call." She picked up the magazine with the craft kit ad in it and walked to the kitchen. She returned a few minutes later. "Your money never arrived at the company warehouse. It could have gotten lost anywhere along the way. I'm afraid you'll have to start saving all over again. You'll also have to be punished for disobeying me."

Valerie nodded silently and went to her bedroom. When she had been punished long enough, Mom came up and put her arm around Valerie. "I think I have an easier way for you to save your money. Come on."

Valerie followed her mom to the basement.

She found a small box and handed it to Valerie. "This can be your offering box. Each day, put aside a part of the money Mrs. Long gives you. Then on Sunday, you'll have your whole offering ready. Why don't you decorate it to make it really special?"

Valerie gathered paper, markers, scissors, and glue and got to work. A short time later, she had a blue offering box decorated with different colored flowers. She opened the lid and put in 40 cents for the four days she'd walked Colby that week. Then she added another 40 cents, the amount she hadn't given the week before.

The next day, Valerie burst into the house after school. "Mrs. Long just asked me to feed Colby and water her plants during the weekend. She's visiting her sister." Valerie gulped some air. "She said she'd pay me $6 for the weekend." She dropped her pack to the floor. "I have to walk Colby. 'Bye." Before Mom could even answer, Valerie had left.

———

That Sunday, Valerie cheerfully placed $1.10 in the offering plate. She and her mom smiled at each other.

A couple days later, Valerie and her mom sat

at the kitchen table. Valerie filled out another order blank that the craft company had sent her. After her mom counted out the right amount of money, she put it in her purse. "Now I'll write out a check for the kit," she said. "No one can cash it except someone from the company."

Valerie grinned. She knew her kit would arrive in a week or so. But Valerie had even more to smile about at the prayer meeting Wednesday evening.

"If you'll all look at the church quarterly financial report," said Rev. Cook at the end of the service, "you'll see that offerings have gone up. In addition to paying salaries, buying new hymnals, and providing for building repairs, we've been able to give more in other areas. We have more money to send to our missionaries, and we've been able to give more to the local food bank." He paused as he turned the page. "And on page two, under educational needs, we bought several new books for the church library. The titles are listed."

Valerie quickly searched through the titles and almost jumped from her seat. The next three books in the Baymont Buddies series had been purchased. They were Valerie's favorite books. Before she left the church, Valerie signed one out.

The next afternoon, after she walked Colby, she put her money in her offering box. Then she eagerly began reading the next adventure of the Baymont Buddies.

The Lightning Escape

Things to Think About

Why was Valerie able to send for the craft kit so soon?

_____

_____

What things happened to Valerie and her money after she sent for the kit the first time?

_____

_____

Who got help from the money given for God's use at her church?

_____

_____

Read Matthew 6:24; 1 Timothy 6:10; Numbers 18:26; Proverbs 11:24 and 28:27. Why should you give a money offering to God?

_____

_____

Read 1 Corinthians 16:1–2 and 2 Corinthians 9:7. How much should each person give and how should he give it?

_____

_____

Read Mark 12:41–44. Why did Jesus say this woman had given more than anyone else if all she gave was a few pennies?

_____

_____

Let's Act It Out!

Memorize Proverbs 11:24.

List ways that God's money is used.

_____

_____

_____

_____

Following the principles of 1 Corinthians 16:1–2, make an offering box or jar. Take a part of your allowance or other earnings and put it in your box as soon as you get it.

4

Easter Brownies

How did we get dragged into this?" asked Roberto as he and the other Fairfield Friends pedaled their bikes slowly through Fairfield Court. They were on their way to the Morgandale Nursing Home. While they rode, Ceely explained the reason for their visit.

"The first through fourth graders at our church had planned this to be an Easter visit since Easter is next Sunday. The four Hodge kids were supposed to come with us, but their plans for Easter changed suddenly. They left this morning for their grandparents' house."

"And the fifth through eighth graders were already supposed to go to the hospital," added Hutch. "That left just me and Ceely."

"Mr. Owens, our youth group leader," continued Ceely, "knows we all help out at Safe

43

Harbor at Christmas. He asked if you'd help us with this. I could hardly say no."

"But that was the homeless shelter," said Cameron. "Nursing homes give me the creeps. Besides, I could have been working on my computer project this afternoon."

"Well, I had to change my visit with my dad," Valerie said. "And we were planning to go for a horseback ride."

"I'm missing a great soccer game," Roberto added.

"I don't mind visiting old folks," said Min. "But the timing wasn't good. I had to miss a ballet class. I'll have to fit an extra one in next week."

They rode in silence the rest of the way. Finally they turned up the drive to the home. After parking their bikes, the friends met Mr. Owens in the lobby.

"Hi ya, kids," he said. "Thanks for coming on such short notice."

The friends nodded politely, and Ceely introduced them to Mr. Owens. Then they followed Mr. Owens down a long hallway to an elevator.

When the doors opened onto the third floor, they were greeted by Nurse Porter. She led them to a large, sunny room at the end of the hall where ten residents waited.

"Everyone has been looking forward to your visit," Nurse Porter said to the group. "I'll be at the nursing desk if you need me," she said as she turned to leave.

"OK, kids," said Mr. Owens. "Let's introduce ourselves to everyone first."

No one moved.

"Well, come on," urged Mr. Owens. "They won't bite."

The friends walked stiffly toward the white-haired ladies and whisker-faced men. Each one tried to talk to the residents, but no one really knew what to say. Finally, Mr. Owens called them back over.

"I don't think things are going too well with you guys doing the talking. I think I'll ask them to talk." Mr. Owens walked into the middle of the room. "Since next week is Easter," he began in a loud voice, "we'd all like to hear about past Easters that you have enjoyed. Who would like to start?"

A frail lady in a wheelchair raised her hand slightly.

"Fine, ma'am. And your name is. . . ?"

"Mrs. Minnie Finch. I was poor when I was a child," she began in a raspy voice. "One Easter, my brothers and sister and I went without new shoes so we could have a ham for Easter dinner. Oh my, what a feast we had. Family and friends from all over came to dinner to celebrate our Savior's resurrection. We were the only family around who had enough food to share with others." She smiled, lost in thought about the Easter dinner of long ago.

"I'd never give up my shoes for a ham," whispered Hutch. "I hate ham."

"Shh," scolded Mr. Owens. "Anybody else?"

"My name is Rose Meade," said a voice from the other side of the room. "I'm 97 years old. I was lucky to come from a family with plenty of money. But my parents always told me that the only true riches come from knowing and serving Jesus Christ. They said, 'Rose, always be ready to sacrifice anything for Him since He gave up His life for you.' I always remembered that and the verse they made me memorize, Ephesians 5:2. 'Live a life of love. Love other people just as Christ loved us. Christ gave himself for us.' "

Rose slowly shifted to the other side of her wheelchair. Her painful arthritis made it difficult to move. "So every Easter service is very joyful for me. Even though I've given up my health, lost my husband and my home, I know those sacrifices are nothing compared to Christ's loving sacrifice for me."

The other residents around her agreed.

A man sitting on a plastic-covered couch near Rose cleared his throat. "I'm Pete," he began loudly. "I can't see or hear so good anymore, but I sure do remember one Easter when I was a boy. There was a bad sickness in the county. Some people died. My ma was always wantin' to help others even if it cost her. She was always quotin' Hebrews 13:16. 'Do not forget to do good to others. And share with them what you have. These are the sacrifices that please God.' "

He cleared his throat again. It echoed throughout the silent room.

"Well, some neighbor children got the sickness. They was real poor and couldn't buy no medicine. So Ma took some of our savings and bought it. She even helped care for them when their parents got sick. Problem was, my ma caught the sickness, too. Oh, she came through it okay, and so did the people she helped. But Ma was expectin' a baby at the time. My baby sister was born dead. Doctors said it was probably the sickness that done it."

The friends shifted their eyes from one to

the other. Min's and Ceely's eyes filled with tears.

"But Ma never blamed the sickness or the children she caught it from or even God. She was always happy that her sacrifice had saved some other children, just as God's sacrifice of His Son saved her soul for heaven. And the next year," added Pete, "Ma gave birth to a healthy boy, my brother Joe."

"That's a wonderful story, Pete," said Mr. Owens. "Thank you for sharing it." He looked at his watch. "I'm afraid it's about time for us to go, though," he said as he stood up. He turned to look at the friends. They motioned to him to come over.

"We'd like to stay longer," said Ceely.

"Yeah," agreed the others.

Mr. Owens grinned. "I'm sure they'll be thrilled."

After the Fairfield Friends sang "Christ the Lord is Risen Today," they talked with the residents, enjoying more of their stories and telling them about themselves. Before long, a tray of brownies arrived for the friends and Mr. Owens.

"Oh, we didn't bring any money along with us," said Mr. Owens.

The Lightning Escape

"You don't need no money," Pete told them.

"We all decided to give up our brownies at lunch today," Minnie said.

"Because you all gave up your time and fun to come see us old folks," added Rose.

An hour later and the brownies eaten, the friends said good-bye to the residents. But they reminded them they'd see them next month. The Fairfield Friends had decided to give up one Saturday a month and spend it with their new friends at the nursing home.

Things to Think About

Why didn't the Fairfield Friends want to go to the nursing home?

_____

_____

What does it mean to sacrifice something? What sacrifices did the nursing home residents tell about?

_____

_____

How did the Fairfield Friends change to sacrifice for others?

_____

_____

Read John 3:16. Why did God sacrifice His Son?

_____

_____

Read Romans 8:32; Titus 2:14; and Hebrews 9:28. What else does God's sacrifice mean for Christians?

_____

_____

The Lightning Escape

Read 2 Corinthians 9:11–13; Ephesians 5:2; and Hebrews 13:16. Why should you sacrifice for others?

_____

_____

Let's Act It Out!

Memorize Hebrews 13:16.

Plan a visit to a nursing home or retirement village near you. Most of them welcome visitors and keep a list of residents who would like to have visitors. Or perhaps your family could plan to visit around a holiday and sing some songs.

Read each example and decide what is the right thing to do. Then talk about what might happen if you don't make a sacrifice.

1. You want to read your book, but your little sister wants you to play a game with her.

2. You need a new winter coat, but since

your dad was laid off at work, your parents want to buy one at a second-hand store. You, however, want to buy a new one from an expensive store.

3. You and your best friend want the best part in a class play. Your friend seems angry that you are competing with him.

4. Some friends are having a slumber party Friday night, and you really want to go. But you know you won't get much sleep and will be tired for an early field hockey game Saturday morning.

5. You've always had your own room, but now that your baby brother was born, your little sister has to move into your room.

6. You're watching your favorite TV show when some friends of your parents stop by. Their toddlers want to watch the *Gonzo Goose Show*.

7. Your classmates want to play some mean tricks on the substitute teacher, which you think aren't right. They say they

won't be friends with you if you don't go along.

8. You're invited to go to an amusement park with some friends all day Sunday, but you know Sunday is God's day and the day you go to church.

9. Your grandma is in the hospital, and your parents insist you go see her with them. But you already had your afternoon planned with other things.

10. A friend asks you to go to a movie on Saturday and you agree to go. Then another friend invites you to go along on a weekend camping trip.

5

Freckles' Close Call

Roberto rolled up the driveway on his bike. He had spent the afternoon swimming with the Fairfield Friends at the Morgandale Community Pool. As Roberto parked his bike, he saw Grandpop putting his dog, Freckles, in his cage.

"Grandpop, what are you doing?" asked Roberto. "Freckles doesn't like being in his cage."

"I'm sure he doesn't, but that's where he's going," Grandpop answered. "Mr. Clepper from three doors down called. Freckles dug up the geraniums his wife just planted."

"Well, he likes to dig and play," said Roberto, defending Freckles.

"There's more," said Grandpop. "After he finished with the geraniums, he chased Mrs.

Carter's cat up a tree . . . again."

"Powderpuff is a scaredy-cat," said Roberto, smiling slightly at his joke.

"This isn't funny anymore," said Grandpop. "Freckles isn't trained and he's disobedient. You need to teach him to obey and punish him when he's bad," Grandpop said firmly.

"But he won't like it if I punish him," said Roberto.

"Look, Roberto, if you truly love Freckles, you'll want to keep him safe by not allowing him to run off." Grandpop paused, then continued. "Now, I saw in the *Morgandale Daily Sentinel* an ad for dog obedience classes. They're being held each morning next week at the community center. I've already signed up you and Freckles."

Roberto sighed but said nothing more. He knew when Grandpop had made up his mind.

———

The following Monday, Roberto put a leash on Freckles. As he headed out the door, Grandpop told him to come straight home after the class.

Roberto plodded out the driveway and turned up the street. Freckles yapped and jumped. He danced and bounced around Roberto's feet. He pulled and strained on the leash, too, almost yanking it out of Roberto's hand.

At the community center, Roberto sat with four other owners and their dogs. The trainer showed them how to give simple commands like "come," "no," and "stop." He also explained how to reward their dogs when they obeyed and how to discipline them when they didn't.

"No!" Roberto yelled at Freckles. "Stop!" he commanded when he walked away. But Freckles wouldn't obey any of the commands. The trainer tried to help, but all Freckles did was jump at Roberto's knees and lick his hand.

As Roberto and Freckles walked home, Brad and Josh rolled up on their bikes.

"Hey," said Brad, "we're playing soccer at the park this afternoon."

"Great," said Roberto. "I'll be there."

"You want to cut over there and see if any games are going on now?" asked Josh.

"Yeah, sure," Roberto answered. They crossed the street and headed for the park.

An hour later, after putting Freckles in his cage, Roberto walked into the house.

"Where have you been?" Grandpop asked, sounding mad.

"I . . . uh . . . went to the park with Brad and Josh," mumbled Roberto.

"I thought I told you to come straight home. I had a doctor's appointment and then needed to go grocery shopping. You know I need your help lifting the bags when Ramone is at work," finished Grandpop, his voice quite loud.

"I guess I forgot," said Roberto. "I'm sorry."

"You also disobeyed me by hanging around with your soccer pals," continued Grandpop. "Have you forgotten about last Halloween?"

Roberto frowned as he thought about how he'd joined in throwing eggs at some houses. He had to repaint Mrs. Thompson's entire garage door. "But they didn't do anything," argued Roberto. "We just went to the park and watched a soccer game."

Grandpop shook his head. "You have to be punished, Roberto. You won't be allowed to go anywhere the rest of the week except to Freckles' obedience classes."

Roberto thought of that afternoon's soccer game. "That's not fair," he said. "I shouldn't be punished for something I forgot."

Grandpop replied, "Hebrews 12:11 says, 'Being punished is painful. But later, after we have learned from being punished . . . we start living in the right way.' "

"You must not love me," continued Roberto.

"Not love you?" said Grandpop. "Are you kidding? 'If a person does not punish his children, he does not love them. But the person who loves his children is careful to correct them.' That's what Proverbs 13:24 says. It's because I *do* love you so much that I know I must train you and discipline you to grow up to be right with God." Grandpop put his hand on Roberto's shoulder and softened his voice. "Now, why don't you go out with Freckles and work on his training."

———

For the next three days, Roberto took Freckles to obedience classes. By Thursday he was angry with Freckles. "He's never going to get it right," Roberto told Grandpop. "He listens a little when I say 'stop,' but then he runs off again."

"Training doesn't happen all at once," explained Grandpop. "You must keep at it. Over time he'll learn those commands and then be able to learn others."

On Friday, the teacher handed out an award to each owner. He gave each dog a bag of doggy treats.

"Well, you didn't learn a whole lot," said Roberto as they walked home. He reached into his bag and held out a doggy treat for Freckles. "But I really don't care. I'm just glad I can go out again tomorrow."

The Lightning Escape

Suddenly, Freckles saw a cat. He yanked hard and fast on the leash, and it flew out of Roberto's hand. Freckles ran after the cat. Roberto chased after Freckles. The cat streaked down Hillside Drive, but when it reached the end of the sidewalk, it didn't stop. The cat ran right across the street.

Roberto saw Freckles reach the corner and run into the street. All at once, a truck appeared. It turned from Wilson Street onto Hillside, right toward Freckles.

"STOP, FRECKLES!" screamed Roberto at the top of his lungs.

Freckles skidded to a stop and looked around. When he saw Roberto, he ran back to him and ran around his ankles and jumped at his knees.

"Oh, Freckles," said Roberto, scooping him up and burying his face in Freckles' neck. "I'm so glad you obeyed. You could have been killed."

"Hey, Roberto. Where have you been?" It was Brad, Josh, and Tony.

"Yeah, you didn't show up for our game on Monday," Josh said.

"We're headed to the park now for another," said Tony.

"Sorry, guys. I can't today. I'm supposed to

go straight home," explained Roberto. "Maybe tomorrow."

Brad laughed at Roberto, and Josh shook his head at him. Then they rode off.

When Roberto got home, he told Grandpop what had happened. "He obeyed me," said Roberto excitedly.

"Looks like that training paid off," said Grandpop.

Roberto nodded and went into the family room to watch a video. Freckles hopped up next to him. Just as the video started, the phone rang. Roberto could hear Grandpop talking in the kitchen. A short time later, he came in and sat down next to Roberto.

"That was Mrs. Thompson. She called because your soccer friends were just caught by the police down the street from her house. They were going through the mailboxes along the street. The police took their names and will call their parents. She was worried you might have been with them." Grandpop smiled. "I told her that you were safe and sound here with me."

"And Freckles," added Roberto.

Freckles licked Roberto's face. Grandpop leaned over and lightly kissed Roberto's head.

The Lightning Escape

Things to Think About

Why were Freckles and Roberto punished?

_____

_____

How did Roberto's training and punishment help Freckles?

_____

_____

How did Grandpop's training and punishment help Roberto?

_____

_____

Read Hebrews 12:6–10. Why does God discipline you?

_____

_____

Read Proverbs 13:24; 22:6; 29:17 and 1 Timothy 3:4. Why do parents and adults discipline you?

_____

_____

Read Proverbs 15:32; Colossians 3:20; and Hebrews 12:11. What do you gain from discipline, training, and being obedient?

_____

_____

Let's Act It Out!

Memorize Hebrew 12:11.

Tape several pieces of white paper together to form a mural. Draw pictures showing the growth, training, and discipline of a dog or cat. For example, you might draw a kitten clawing the furniture, then a picture with a person showing the kitten how to use a scratch pad. Finally, you could draw an older cat using the scratch pad on its own.

Now do the same thing with a boy or girl, showing some kind of training or learning (example: baby being fed, toddler using fingers, child using spoon). Be sure to include spiritual growth, too. You could draw a child looking at a Bible picture book, followed by a picture of him sitting in church. Then you could show him telling a friend about Jesus. Now come up with your own ideas. Be creative!

6

Tree House Disaster

O ur tree house sure will be cool when it's done," said Cameron as he pulled a rope through the slot of a pulley.

"You said it," added Hutch.

"I'll bet no one ever had a tree house this awesome," finished Roberto as he stirred a can of paint.

The three boys, along with Mr. Coleman and Mr. Parker, had built a tree house in some woods on the edge of Morgandale. A man who worked with Cameron's dad owned the land and had said they could build it.

"We should be done in a couple more days," said Hutch.

"We just have the painting to finish," Roberto added. After dipping his brush into the can, he slapped some green paint on the walls.

"And I need to get the pulley working," said Cameron. He had made a rope-and-pulley system so they could pull things up in a basket on the end of a rope.

"I sure am thankful God provided us with the wood we needed," Roberto said.

"What do you mean?" asked Cameron. "The wood was left over from building the Miller house. Mr. Miller gave it to us. And we already thanked him for it."

"But God made it happen," said Hutch.

"Yeah," agreed Roberto. "My grandpop says we should thank God for everything."

Cameron shrugged and continued working on his pulley. Hutch and Roberto painted quietly.

A while later, Roberto looked at his watch. "Hey, I have to go. It's almost 5:30."

"Aww," said Cameron. "I'm almost done with this. Are we coming back tomorrow to work?"

"We can't," said Roberto. "Hutch and I have baseball practice in the morning."

"And a game in the afternoon," Hutch added.

"Oh, all right," Cameron replied. "I'll meet you back here on Wednesday."

After climbing down the rope ladder, they

hopped on their bikes and pedaled toward Fairfield Court.

Ten minutes later, Cameron parked his bike in the garage and entered the house. "I'm home," he yelled.

"You're late," said Mom. "Dinner was ready five minutes ago."

"Sorry," said Cameron, sitting down at the table with the rest of the family.

"Let's pray," said Dad. "Lord, we give you great thanks for the food you've provided. And we especially give thanks for bringing Uncle Monte through his surgery. May you continue to heal him. Amen."

"Isn't that wonderful news about Uncle Monte?" Mom said as she passed a plate of chicken.

"How long does he have to stay in the hospital?" asked Cameron's older brother, Philip.

"A few more days, I think," Dad answered. "But God will see him through it."

"I don't get it," said Cameron, putting down his fork. "What's God got to do with Uncle Monte's heart surgery and recovery? I mean, the doctors did the surgery and gave him the medicine he needs."

Before anyone could answer, Cameron

continued in a rush, "It's just like with saying grace before we eat. We have food because Dad has a job and brings home a paycheck. And Mom gets the groceries at the store and cooks the food."

"But, Cameron," answered Dad, "God has given me the job."

"And God brings rain and sun for the farmers who grow our food. He also is responsible for the knowledge used to make and package foods," added Mom.

"Colossians 3:17 says, 'And in all you do, give thanks to God the Father through Jesus,'" said Dad. "Everything comes by way of God, Cameron," he explained. "So we should thank Him for everything."

Cameron sighed and shook his head. He picked up his fork and continued eating.

The next day, Cameron surfed the Internet for a while on his computer. But he soon got bored. *I really want to work on that pulley*, he thought. *I guess there's no reason I can't work on it today and get it finished. Then tomorrow I can help Hutch and Roberto paint.*

After arriving at the tree house, Cameron climbed up the rope ladder and onto the floor of the house. He picked up the rope and pulley, but as he did, Cameron tripped over the rope and fell right through the open door. He landed on the ground below with a thud, his head hitting a rock.

Cameron lay there a minute, too stunned to move. His head pounded horribly. He felt his forehead and realized he was bleeding a lot. Cameron tried to sit up, but he was so dizzy he fell back again.

What should I do? thought Cameron. *I'm too dizzy to ride home or even walk. But I need to stop this bleeding and get help. I must have hurt my head badly.*

All at once Cameron remembered some-

thing his gym teacher had told them during first-aid week at school. He pulled off his sneaker, slid off his long tube sock, and wrapped it snugly around his head. The bleeding slowed down.

Now I need to get help. Cameron looked around. He saw the mirror on his bike and had an idea. He crawled over to his bike and unscrewed the mirror. Then he pointed it toward the sun. The sun's rays gleamed brightly on the mirror as he wiggled it. *Now if someone on the road would just see the flashing light.*

But after a while, Cameron's arm got tired, his head hurt more, and he felt even dizzier. He put the mirror down. The trees above him began to spin around. He closed his eyes.

"Cameron, Cameron!"

Who's calling me? he wondered, not fully awake.

"Cameron, wake up!" Roberto yelled.

Hutch shook him gently.

Cameron opened his eyes to slits. "What are you guys doing here?"

"We were on our way home from practice for lunch and we saw this bobbing light in the woods," explained Roberto.

"We thought someone might be messing

around with the tree house," said Hutch, "so we rode over."

"What happened?" asked Roberto.

"I fell through the door," Cameron answered. "I'm really dizzy."

"I'll go for help," Hutch said. He jumped on his bike and took off.

"I'll stay with you until help comes," said Roberto.

———

An hour later, Cameron lay in a hospital bed. His family and Hutch and Roberto were talking with him when a doctor walked in.

"Well, you're doing better," he said. He picked up Cameron's chart at the foot of the bed. "Needed four stitches to close up that cut. It's a good thing you knew how to stop the bleeding." He turned to Mr. and Mrs. Parker. "Since he did bang his head rather hard, we'd like to keep an eye on him overnight. But he'll be fine."

Mr. and Mrs. Parker nodded. "Thank you," said Mr. Parker.

"Oh, don't thank me," he said. "It's the boys who should be thanked for getting help quickly."

"We're just thankful Cameron knew how to

signal with his mirror," said Roberto.

"And we're especially thankful we happened to be riding home at the right time," added Hutch.

"But I'm thankful to God," said Cameron, "because He's the one who made all those things work out." He smiled at his parents and then at Hutch and Roberto. The boys walked over to Cameron, then they all slapped their hands together in a high five.

The Lightning Escape

Things to Think About

What things didn't Cameron want to thank God for? Why didn't he want to thank God?

_____

_____

_____

_____

What happened to Cameron while he was at the tree house alone?

_____

_____

What things did Cameron finally thank God for?

_____

_____

Read Psalm 100, 103:1–5, and 118:28–29; Philippians 4:19; and 1 John 5:11. Why should you give thanks to God?

_____

_____

Read Psalm 30:12; Mark 8:16; and Colossians 2:6–7 and 3:17. When, how often, and how much should you thank God?

_____

_____

Let's Act It Out

Make a list of things you're thankful for. Be sure to include some of these in your prayers each day.

_____

_____

_____

_____

Draw a picture of something you're thankful for.

Make a family "thankfulness" collage. Cut pictures out of old magazines that show what your family is thankful for. Place them on a piece of construction paper or cardboard. Then glue them on.

7

An October Christmas

We're home," called Min. She and Valerie walked into the kitchen. "Want some milk and cookies?" she asked.

"Sure," answered Valerie.

"Hello, dear," Grandmother Hing said to Min, walking into the kitchen. "How nice to see you again, Valerie. I hear you are spending the night with Min."

"Yes, ma'am," said Valerie, using her most formal voice with Grandmother Hing.

"Min, your mother called to say she would be late from work. But she will pick up pepperoni pizzas for supper and rent the video you wanted."

"Yes!" Min and Valerie cheered together.

That evening, after every piece of pizza had been eaten, Mr. Hing placed his Bible on the table. "We've been working through Proverbs for our family devotions," he said to Valerie. He pushed aside an empty pizza box and slid his Bible over to Min. "Min, would you read Proverbs 19:17, please?"

Min began. " 'Being kind to the poor is like lending to the Lord. The Lord will reward you for what you have done.' "

"What do you think?" Mr. Hing asked. "How can we give to the poor?"

"Doesn't some of our weekly church offering go to the poor?" asked Min.

"And sometimes we donate your outgrown clothing," said Mrs. Hing.

"I can think of one more way," said Grandmother. "We can be kind by treating needy people with respect. We should not make fun of them or treat them differently from others."

The following Monday, Min and Valerie walked to Fairfield Elementary together. After the bell rang, they hurried down the long hall toward their rooms.

As Min entered her room, she saw a new girl sitting at a desk. As Min and her classmates took their seats, they all stared at the girl. She had a hole in the front of her shirt, and her sneakers were old canvas ones. They had holes in them, too. A couple girls pointed to them and snickered.

"Let's welcome Teresa Kelly," said Mrs. Stake. "Teresa, could you tell us a little about yourself, maybe where you're from?"

"I'm from down South," said Teresa with an accent. "But no place is really home. My family will be in town for just a few weeks. We're migrant workers."

An uneasy moment passed before Mrs. Stake explained that migrant workers moved from place to place picking apples or other fruit.

The Peters, who owned some apple orchards outside Morgandale, planted more and more trees every year. This fall, for the first time, they hired migrant families to help with the picking. It was clear to everyone that migrant workers didn't make much money.

During recess, Min told Valerie about Teresa. They watched her walk over to one of the first-grade girls.

"Bet that's her sister," Valerie said.

"Her shirt is way too small, and her bangs are so long they hang in her eyes," Min said sadly.

"Yeah," Valerie agreed. "Her socks don't even match."

"Look how those kids are laughing at them," said Min.

She and Valerie kept an eye on Teresa and her sister during the rest of recess. They also made plans.

At lunch, Min saw some kids whisper to each other and roll their eyes when Teresa walked in. Others pointed at her and giggled. Min found Valerie in the cafeteria line. Their eyes locked. Then they nodded.

After Min picked up her lunch, she walked right over to Teresa's table and sat down. Valerie joined her a short time later. Out of the corners of their eyes, they saw the stares of their friends.

"Hi," said Min. "My name is Min, and this is my friend Valerie."

"Hi," Teresa said to Valerie. "This is my little sister, Annie."

"Hi, Annie," Valerie said.

Annie smiled shyly.

"Would you two like to come over after school?" Min asked.

Teresa and Annie looked at each other. "We can't," said Teresa. "We have to work in the orchards. Sunday is our only day off."

"Oh," said Min weakly. She changed the

subject, and they talked about school until the end of lunch.

Back in her classroom, Min's classmates pretended she wasn't even there. At recess, Min and Valerie joined Teresa and Annie. But no one would let them join in any games.

After school, Valerie stopped in at Min's house. They told Grandmother about Teresa and Annie and about what had happened.

"I'm very proud of you both," Grandmother said. "You really put into practice what we talked about Friday night."

"Yeah, I guess," Min said softly.

"But we want to do more," Valerie said eagerly. "Do you think we could give them some money so they can get some new clothes?"

"That is a nice thought, Valerie," answered Grandmother. "But needy people usually do not want a handout. They like to earn their money like anybody else."

Min and Valerie walked silently onto the front porch. They had no idea how Teresa and Annie could earn money.

Just then a car pulled up next to the telephone pole in front of the house. They watched a woman nail a large sign to it. It announced a weekend neighborhood yard sale at some homes in Fairfield Court. After Min and Valerie talked briefly, they ran back into the house to find Grandmother.

That Sunday afternoon, Mr. Hing drove Min and Valerie outside Morgandale to the apple orchards. They picked up Teresa and Annie for the afternoon. After they played some games, they put on a puppet show. Then Min and Valerie winked at each other.

"Let's go play in the leaves," said Valerie quite loudly.

When they got outside, Grandmother Hing appeared. "Would you four like to earn a little spending money?" she asked.

They all nodded.

"Well, after you are done playing in the leaves, you can rake them up and put them in bags. I will give you each a dollar."

First the four friends jumped in the leaves. Next, they buried each other. Finally, they raked them up and stuffed them into bags.

"Hey, I know where we can get a lot for our money," said Min after Grandmother had paid them.

"Just follow us," said Valerie excitedly. They all took off running down the street.

At the first yard sale they came to, Teresa

The Lightning Escape

and Annie each picked out a shirt. They cost ten cents apiece.

"You know what?" said Teresa to Annie. "We could buy presents for Mom, Dad, and Jimmy and save them for a couple months until Christmas."

While Teresa and Annie looked for gifts for their family, Min and Valerie sneaked next door to another yard sale. They whispered as they walked.

Before long, Teresa and Annie had spent all their money. But they were happy with what they had bought: shirts for everyone, a cooking pan for Mom, a hammer for Dad, and a truck for three-year-old Jimmy.

Min and Valerie appeared suddenly. Min had two pairs of socks, a bag of barrettes, and a sweater. Valerie held a pair of leather sneakers, a jacket, and a deck of cards.

"Here, these are for you," Min said, smiling.

"Oh, our parents don't allow us to accept charity or handouts," Teresa said.

"This isn't charity," Valerie burst out. "These are our early Christmas presents to you!"

Teresa and Annie smiled. "Thanks," they said.

Teresa sat down and put on her new sneakers. They fit perfectly. Min helped Annie put some barrettes in her hair. She looked really cute.

Then they walked back to the Hing house, singing Christmas carols all the way.

The Lightning Escape

Things to Think About

What did Min and Valerie learn about kindness?

_____

_____

_____

How were Min and Valerie kind to Teresa and Annie?

_____

_____

_____

How did they arrange for Teresa and Annie to earn money?

_____

_____

_____

Read Proverbs 14:21, 31. What good things happen when you are kind to the needy?

_____

_____

_____

Read Matthew 6:2–4. What should you be careful of?

_____

_____

_____

Read Ephesians 4:32a and 1 Thessalonians 5:15. Who else should you be kind to?

_____

_____

_____

Read Genesis 39:20–23 and Acts 14:17. How does God show kindness to His people?

_____

_____

_____

Let's Act It Out!

Memorize Ephesians 4:32a.

Write a kindness poem using each letter in the word to begin a sentence of a kind act you could do. For example:

The Lightning Escape

K   —*K*eep a promise to a friend
I   —*I*nvite a new classmate over to play

Now come up with your own ideas and finish the whole word.

_____

_____

_____

_____

_____

_____

_____

Bake some "kindness" cookies. Bake sugar cookies (the kind you find in your grocery store's dairy case are easy to make). When cool, decorate with smiley faces using small tubes of icing. Take them to a shelter in your area, to an older church member, or new neighbors. Be sure to stay awhile and visit with them. Perhaps you could invite them to church.

8

Winners Without Winning

"Did you guys hear about the public TV video contest?" Cameron asked Hutch and Roberto as he rolled a snowball for the snowman they were building.

"You mean the one they have every year and the winning video gets put on TV?" asked Roberto. He helped Cameron lift the head onto the body.

"Yeah, that's the one," Cameron said, nodding. "I wanted to enter it last year. I had some good ideas. But I always get too nervous to be in front of the camera when they film it." He stuck a carrot in the middle of the head.

"You sound like Ceely," said Hutch, "only in reverse. She says she likes to perform and can write the report that goes with the project. But she says she never comes up with any good ideas." Hutch placed two rocks above the nose for eyes.

"Ceely wants to enter the video contest?" asked Cameron.

"That's all she talks about," Hutch answered. "There," he said, grinning at the finished snowman. "You know, he sort of looks like my bus driver."

———

Later that day, Cameron called Ceely. After supper, she joined Cameron in the basement of his home. Cameron had his computer set up there and a whole bunch of science stuff.

"Since the theme is 'Celebrate Spring,' I thought we could do something on animals in the spring," suggested Cameron. "We could show them coming out of their winter sleep, having babies and stuff."

"That's a great idea," said Ceely. "But how do we show all that?"

After turning on his computer, Cameron hit some buttons and clicked the mouse. Almost instantly, pictures of animals appeared on the screen.

"The computer can copy these pictures onto a clear, plastic sheet to use on an overhead projector. It casts the picture onto a movie screen and makes it larger. I can also do animal sounds on CD." Cameron stuck a compact disc in the slot, and a bear growled. Ceely jumped and then laughed.

"This is awesome. But what do I do?"

Cameron typed in b-e-a-r. A picture of a black bear appeared and with it some facts about the bear.

"You can get information on each animal out of the encyclopedia I have on disc or from other books at the library," Cameron explained. "Then just write a report on each animal. You read while I work the projector and animal recordings."

The following Saturday, Cameron's dad drove them to the TV station. They would be there all day since each person or group had to have their presentation filmed.

Shortly after Cameron and Ceely joined some other kids in the filming studio, a woman entered.

"Attention, please," she yelled. "I'm Mrs. Martz, the program director. Please come to this table and sign in with your projects."

She had barely finished her sentence when the others charged toward the table.

"I'm first!" yelled a boy with red hair as he clawed his way to the front of the line. He shoved a girl away from him.

"But you just got here," said the girl.

"She didn't say you had to sign up in the order you came," Redhead said back. He held his ground while the others fought for position behind him. Cameron and Ceely lined up after all of them. They were eleventh in line.

"This is going to take forever," said the two girls in front of them.

"It's not fair," whined a boy behind them who'd just arrived. "Waiting will be so boring."

After signing in, Cameron and Ceely sat quietly in some chairs along the wall. While the others ran all around the room, Ceely and Cameron played a game of cards.

Suddenly, they heard a crash. Two kids bolted away from the camera they had knocked over. Cameron and Ceely could both see the large sign attached to it that said, "DO NOT TOUCH."

A few minutes later, the camera man and Mrs. Martz entered the room. "We're ready to begin filming," she said.

"I don't think so," said the camera man when he saw the camera lying on the floor. "It doesn't look broken, but it will have to be completely reset."

"That means we won't be ready for a

while," said Mrs. Martz.

"Aww," said most of the kids.

"How long will it be?" yelled the redhead.

"Do we still get the same amount of time to do our videos?" shouted a girl.

"What if we mess up?" asked the whiny boy. "Do we get to go again?"

While Mrs. Martz tried to answer their questions, Ceely leaned over and whispered to Cameron, "All of this made me remember the Bible verse I memorized for school last week. Philippians 2:5. 'In your lives you must think and act like Christ Jesus.' "

Cameron laughed softly. "I guess you mean this reminds you of the opposite of that verse."

Ceely nodded.

Half an hour later, Mrs. Martz called the first group over to the filming area. Two girls kept arguing over who was to do what.

"You'd think they'd have decided that before now," said Ceely.

"All they have to do is share the parts," Cameron said.

Another group kept rehearsing and used up most of their filming time.

"It's not fair," said a girl with braids. "We should get more time."

Slowly, the numbers inched their way

toward Cameron and Ceely. While number nine was filming, Ceely quietly read through her report. Cameron checked his equipment. When they were called, they set up, rehearsed twice, then filmed their three-minute video.

"I'll be viewing these with the other judges," said Mrs. Martz as she collected the videos. "Then I'll be back to announce the winner."

When she returned, the room became quiet for the first time. Everyone held their breath as Mrs. Martz spoke. "In second place, for their video about animals in the spring, are Ceely Coleman and Cameron Parker. Let's have a round of applause for the runners-up."

Ceely and Cameron grinned at each other. They didn't hear anybody clap, though, only some whispering nearby about their video not being very good.

"And now for the winner," continued Mrs. Martz, "who showed us different types of spring flowers and where they grow best. Tommy Booth."

The redheaded boy jumped up on his chair. He made a V with his fingers for a victory sign and waved them in the air. Ceely and Cameron clapped, but no one else did.

"Well, we may not have won," said

Cameron as he and Ceely waited outside for Mr. Parker to come. "But it was a great time."

"It sure was," agreed Ceely. "I might become a news reporter someday. I really liked reading in front of the camera."

"Excuse me," said someone behind them. It was the camera man. "I've been watching you two all day. You may not have won the contest, but you'll both be winners in life."

"What do you mean?" asked Cameron.

The camera man explained. "You both behaved well all day while everyone else's behavior and attitudes were rotten."

———

Two weeks later, letters arrived for both Ceely and Cameron from Mrs. Martz. She wrote that the station had discovered that Tommy Booth had copied his project from an older sister who'd won six years earlier. Ceely and Cameron's video had become the winner. It would run on TV several times over the next three months.

On Saturday evening, the Fairfield Friends gathered at the Parkers' house for the first showing of the video. They clapped and cheered for Ceely and Cameron's winning video.

"Thanks," said Ceely.

"But we were winners even before we won," finished Cameron.

Ceely and Cameron laughed at the others' confused looks. Then they explained what they meant.

The Lightning Escape

Things to Think About

What is "attitude"?

_____

_____

In what ways did the kids at the TV station
show a poor attitude? How did Cameron and
Ceely show a good attitude?

_____

_____

What were the two ways that Ceely and
Cameron were winners?

_____

_____

Read Philippians 2:14–15 and Hebrews 4:13.
Why should you have a good attitude?

_____

_____

Read Philippians 2:5 and Ephesians 4:22–24.
Who should you model your attitude after?

_____

_____

Read Titus 2:7–8. What else results from your
good attitude?

_____

_____

Let's Act It Out!

Memorize Philippians 2:14.

Play this "luck-of-the-draw" game called Good and Bad Attitudes. Number slips of paper from 1–12. Take turns drawing a number and reading that situation out loud to the others. Talk about why some situations are worth fewer points than others. What are some ways to solve the 0-point situations using a good attitude?

1. You and a friend are playing cards, and your friend wins the game. You tell him he cheated and angrily stomp off. 0 points

2. You're at a restaurant with your family. As you wait for your food, you keep whining and complaining about having to wait. 0 points

3. You ask your parents if you can ride your bike in the street. They say no because it's too dangerous on the busy street you live on. Though you're sad, you accept their answer because you know they care about your safety. 2 points

4. You were planning to go swimming with some friends, but it rained so you sit inside the house all day and mope around. 0 points

5. Your mom has a doctor's appointment and you have to go along. You don't complain to her about having to go. Since you know you'll have to wait for a while, you take a book along to read. While your mom is seeing the doctor, you sit quietly. 3 points

6. You got an A on a test and no one else did. You brag to everyone about it at recess. 0 points

7. You're shopping with your family and you start to get tired. You fuss that you want to go home and don't want to shop for anyone else. 0 points

8. At a carnival there is free face painting. There are ten people ahead of you in line. You wait calmly until your turn. 1 point

9. You and your brother start arguing over a toy. You suggest you both take turns using it and let him go first. 2 points

10. You didn't get the grade you think you should have gotten on a book report. You complain to your teacher about it and then to your friends on the bus. 0 points

11. You're being punished by your parents for something you did and can't watch TV for a week. You stay angry at everyone, including your friends, all week. 0 points

12. You try out for the lead in the school play but don't get the part. You tell the person who did "good job." 1 point

9

An Honest B

Oh no," Ceely whispered to herself. "It can't be." Ceely checked the name and grade twice on her math paper. She was sure she wasn't seeing them right. But she was. A big red C+ sat on the page. The name at the top said Ceely Coleman.

Although math was her hardest subject, Ceely always got an A on her report card by doing extra-credit problems.

Ceely's eyes watered. She knew all the extra credit in the world wouldn't change a C+ to an A. *My only chance*, thought Ceely, *is to get an A+ on the final math test of the year.*

After supper, Ceely showed her parents her test. "I didn't read the directions right for one part," she quickly explained. "But I can still get an A on my report card. I know I can. I'll study really hard."

"Whoa, slow down, Ceely," said Dad. "We aren't upset about your grade. We know you did your best."

"And we never said you have to get straight As," Mom added.

"But I want all As," Ceely said.

"We know," said Dad. "But it won't be the end of the world if you get a B on your report card."

Ceely sighed as she left the room. She slowly hiked the steps to her bedroom and flopped onto her bed. *It will too be the end of the world if I get a B*, she thought. *I'll just have to make sure I get an A.* Ceely reached down and picked up her math book and began to practice some problems.

———

During the next few days, Ceely used all her spare time to work on her math. On Saturday afternoon, though, she took a break and decided to listen to her new cassette tape. Her mom had picked up the next one in the Christian Character series at the Hosanna Christian Book Store. Ceely read the title on the case. "Self-control."

The Lightning Escape

The story was about a boy whose father sold candy to grocery stores. He usually had broken pieces left in the bottom of boxes that couldn't be sold in the stores. His boss let the workers buy the pieces at a lower price and take them home to their families.

Ten-year-old Kyle wanted to be a salesman like his dad. After paying his dad for some candy from his allowance, he set up a "store" on the front porch. Using his dad's scale, Kyle weighed the candy and sold it to neighborhood kids. He made a nice profit on the candy.

But then Kyle, tempted to get more money, set the scale higher. When it read one pound, the real weight was only a half pound. But Kyle charged all the kids for a full pound.

One day, Kyle's dad saw how much money he had made. It seemed way too much. The next day, his dad watched him sell candy from the living room window. He saw that the scale marker had been moved up.

"You're cheating your customers with dishonest scales," said his dad. "Amos 8:5 says, '. . . we can bring out wheat to sell. We can charge them more and give them less. We can change the scales to cheat the people.' You were dishonest by taking more money than was owed to you. That's a form of cheating.

First Peter 5:8 says, 'Control yourselves and be careful.' You sinned because you didn't control yourself."

Kyle's dad made him give back half of all the money to the kids who'd bought candy. Although he didn't like the idea at first, afterward he actually felt much better.

Ceely liked the story. She liked the verse in 1 Peter, too, since it was easy to remember.

————

After school on Monday, Ceely and Hutch met up with Roberto as they walked home from their bus stop.

"We have to pick up a loaf of bread," said Hutch, heading into the small grocery store a block from their house. Hutch picked up the loaf of bread. It cost $1.50. He handed the clerk a five-dollar bill. The clerk gave him $4.50 in change.

Roberto nudged Hutch and whispered to him, "He gave you an extra dollar in change. Why don't you buy a couple of candy bars or something?"

Hutch nudged Ceely. "Look." He showed her the change. "He gave back too much money. We can split it and buy something for ourselves."

The Lightning Escape

Ceely stopped. "Hutch, that's not right." She frowned at Roberto. "The money belongs to the store. First Peter 5:8 says, 'Control yourselves and be careful.' You have to watch out for temptations to sin, like cheating, and then control yourself not to do it."

Hutch sighed. "Oh, all right." He walked back to the clerk. "Excuse me," he said, "but you gave me too much change." Hutch handed him a dollar.

"Why, thank you," said the clerk. "My wife is in the hospital, so I haven't been paying attention to my work very well."

"Now don't you feel better?" Ceely asked when they got outside.

"I guess," Hutch answered. "But a candy bar would have felt good in my mouth."

———

For the next two weeks, Ceely continued to practice math problems. She really wanted that A+. Before she knew it, though, the day of the big test arrived.

"Class, you'll be taking your math test in the multipurpose room right after lunch," announced Mrs. Horner. "Second and third graders will be meeting in there as well to take tests. Then, after everyone is done, the teachers will show a movie to all three grades.''

''Hurray!'' yelled Ceely along with her classmates. She joined in the whispering as they wondered what movie it would be.

After all the classes arrived in the multipurpose room, the teachers passed out the tests to their students. Ceely worked carefully through the difficult math test, but three problems stumped her. She had answers, but she wasn't sure they were right.

Bill, sitting next to her, usually got perfect papers in math. Slowly, Ceely shifted her eyes to the right. After looking at Bill's paper, she quickly erased her answers and put down his.

Ceely checked over the rest of her paper. She was ready to turn it in when she heard someone pass by and whisper, ''First Peter 5:8. 'Control yourselves and be careful.' ''

Ceely froze. It was Hutch. *He must have been watching me.* Ceely looked at her paper a long time. Finally, she erased the three answers and put her original answers back. Then she turned in her paper.

Ceely and Hutch didn't talk about what had happened. But on Monday, when Ceely showed Hutch her B+ on her test, he smiled at her. ''Now don't you feel better?''

Ceely nodded but sighed heavily.

The following week, school was over for the year. Ceely and Hutch arrived home with their report cards. When Mom saw Ceely's B in math, she waited for Ceely to look really sad about it.

When Ceely didn't say anything, Mom patted her on the back. "I guess it's tough getting a B, isn't it?"

"Oh, not really," answered Ceely. "I've never been happy with a B before, but I am this time."

A Fairfield Friends Devotional Adventure

Mom frowned at her in a puzzled way.

Ceely and Hutch looked at each other and laughed. Then they ran outside to begin their summer vacations.

The Lightning Escape

Things to Think About

Why did Ceely change her answers on her math test?

_____

_____

Why did she change them back?

_____

_____

What three examples of cheating were shown in the story?

_____

_____

Read Proverbs 11:1 and 20:23. What does God think about cheating?

_____

_____

Read Ephesians 6:10–18 and Titus 2:11–12. Who tempts you to cheat and helps you to lose self-control?

_____

_____

How can you regain or keep your self-control?

_____

_____

Read 1 Peter 3:11–14, 17. Why is it better to control yourself and not cheat, even if it means things won't work out in the way you want?

_____

_____

Let's Act It Out!

Memorize 1 Peter 5:8.

Number slips of paper from 1–12. As each person draws a number, he or she must tell what's the right thing to do in that situation.

1. You're playing a card game with some friends. You lean forward to change your position and look at the others' cards.

2. You don't know the answer to number four on your social studies test so you peek at your neighbor's paper.

3. You are to read a book for school but decide to watch the video instead.

4. You buy a double-dip cone for 95 cents and give the store clerk a dollar. He gives you a quarter in change instead of a nickel.

5. While your teacher is reviewing the test that was just returned to you, you find a wrong answer that she didn't mark as wrong. You know that one more wrong will drop your grade from an A to a B.

6. At a swim meet, one of the girls on your team on the 10-and-under freestyle relay is sick. The coach tells Cassie, who is 11, to swim in your relay.

7. You forgot to do your homework so you copy it on the bus from a classmate.

8. You are to walk your neighbor's dog each day for half an hour, for which you receive 50 cents. You always stop and talk to friends and then return to the house after half an hour. But the dog receives only 5–10 minutes of exercise.

9. You are to do a report on worms using several books and then write it in your own words. You use one book and copy the report word for word from the book.

10. You plan to sell your old cassette player at the yard sale your mom is having. When someone asks why it doesn't play, you tell him it just needs new batteries when you know there is something else wrong with it.

11. Your parents gave you extra money for Sunday school so you can give to the special missionary fund. When the basket is passed to you, you just pretend to put the money in.

12. You tell your little sister you'll give her 50 cents for making your bed. Since she doesn't know anything about money, you give her five pennies.

10

The Lightning Escape

The last day of vacation Bible school had arrived at Ceely and Hutch's church. The Fairfield Friends had all attended. Seated in the pews with their classes, they waited for the class presentations to begin.

"I know you've all studied the Old Testament men of faith this week," said Pastor Sherman. "So let's have Mrs. Peterson's class start and show us all what they've learned."

Hutch and Valerie filed up front with the others in their class. "We learned about Noah," said Hutch, "and how he had faith in God to build an ark."

"He also had faith that God would take the flood away," added Kim, a classmate.

Ryan and Caitlin held up pictures they'd drawn with Noah on the ark.

"We also learned about Daniel," said Valerie, stepping forward. "He had faith that God would keep him safe from the lions when the king's men threw him in the den."

The next class included Min and Cameron. Cameron read from the Bible about Abraham's faith in Hebrews 11:11 and 12. " 'He was too old to have children, and Sarah was not able to have children,' " read Cameron. " 'It was by faith that Abraham was made able to become a father. . . . From him came as many descendants as there are stars in the sky.' "

The rest of the class acted out the faith of Moses. Tom Tallman raised his hands in the air and pretended to part the Red Sea. Some others walked over some flattened cardboard boxes that served as dry land. The soldiers began running after them. Min and Tracy threw buckets of blue construction paper on them, pretending it was the sea falling back down.

Finally, Roberto and Ceely's class sang a song about Joshua. He had faith that the walls of Jericho would fall down so they could capture the city.

The class next told the story of Gideon's faith that God would help him defeat the Midianites. Roberto and two others blew on toy trumpets while Ceely read from Judges

7:22. " 'When Gideon's 300 men blew their trumpets, the Lord caused all the men of Midian to fight each other with their swords!' " More kids ran to the center and began fighting each other with cardboard swords. " 'The enemy army ran away,' " finished Ceely.

When the presentations were over, the Fairfield Friends rode their bikes back to Fairfield Court. Before they each went their own way, they agreed to meet after supper for a softball game.

At 7 P.M. the friends met at the vacant lot by the old shoe factory. They chose up sides and began the game. They battled back and forth with hits, pop flies, strikes, and stolen bases. The friends were so involved in their game that they didn't see the dark clouds piling up in the sky. They didn't even notice when the sun disappeared.

Suddenly, a bolt of jagged lightning cut through the sky. Min jumped. Valerie shrieked. And then a huge clap of thunder exploded right over them. Before the friends knew what was happening, the thunderstorm was upon them.

"We'll never make it home," said Roberto as heavy rain poured down.

"We need to take cover," Ceely said. She

looked at the empty factory on the other side of the vacant lot. "The shoe factory!" she shouted above the whistling wind. "C'mon!"

By the time they reached the door, they were soaked. "It's locked!" yelled Hutch who had gotten there first.

"Try the other door!" screamed Valerie. They ran to it, but it also had a lock. Cameron and Roberto pulled with all their strength. The rusted lock broke, the door flew open, and the six friends scrambled inside.

Just as the door closed behind them, an ear-splitting crack of thunder filled the air. The Fairfield Friends turned and looked out a window. Just as they did, a knife of lightning stabbed an old tree next to the factory. The tree snapped and slowly toppled, the top of it falling against the door.

Cameron and Roberto pushed on the door, but it wouldn't move. "The tree must be tight against it," said Roberto. "It won't budge."

They tried the window. But it was locked and too heavy to break.

"Just great," Valerie said. "Now what do we do?"

"I sure hope we don't have to spend the night in here," said Cameron.

"We'll be OK," offered Min.

"Sure," agreed Ceely. "Someone will come along and find us."

"Maybe we should build an ark," suggested Hutch.

"Don't make jokes," said Cameron.

"Who's joking?" Hutch asked as buckets of rain poured down.

"I don't think an ark is the answer," said Roberto. "But Noah and the other men of faith we learned about can help."

The others looked at him silently. "Oh yeah," said Valerie suddenly. "We should have faith like Daniel and Moses."

"And Joshua and Abraham," added Min.

"And Gideon," finished Ceely.

"I guess someone will find us," agreed Cameron.

"Or else God will show us a way out," Roberto said. "But it's too dark to look now. We should just find a comfortable, safe place until someone does come."

The Fairfield Friends felt their way along a wall. Roberto tripped over an old canvas cover of some sort. They sat down along the wall and pulled the cover over them. Outside the storm raged. Jagged lightning ripped the sky. The wind roared like a train as it whipped around the corner of the building.

"Look at that," said Cameron. "The lightning flashes shined right through that window down there. I never heard of lightning doing that."

"It's just like that strange, loud thunder that started," said Min. "It feels like it's pounding to get in here."

They all huddled closer under the canvas. But they weren't scared. After a quick prayer in which each asked God to help them have faith, they drifted off to sleep.

When they awoke, it was morning and the

sun was shining. "C'mon," said Roberto, throwing off the cover. "It's time to find a way out."

They walked through the huge factory, checking all the doors. They were all locked. Suddenly, they heard rustling behind them. They turned, and there stood a silver tabby cat with a dead mouse dangling from her mouth.

"Yuk!" said Min, wrinkling her face.

"Oh, gross," agreed Valerie.

"Fantastic!" exclaimed Cameron. "If she caught a mouse and brought it in here, there must be a way out."

The cat turned and trotted off. The six friends followed her to the other end of the building. They watched her leap up on crates and boxes and through an open window. It was very small, but Hutch, after climbing up the boxes like the cat, slid through the window.

———

Half an hour later, two policemen with an electric saw had cut through the tree at the door. Parents, friends, and neighbors rolled away the piece of trunk. The Fairfield Friends burst through the door and into their families' arms. The whole neighborhood and many others from Morgandale turned out for the happy celebration. Many had feared something awful had happened to the children.

Nearby, a policeman talked with his captain. "I don't understand," the friends heard him say. "I checked here last night," he said. "I shined my flashlight in the window and pounded on the door with my club. But I didn't see anyone, and no one came."

The friends looked at each other and laughed, realizing what had happened. They walked over to the policeman and explained that they thought he was just part of the thunderstorm.

Suddenly a reporter ran up and snapped their picture. "I'm doing a story on you kids for the *Morgandale Daily Sentinel*," he said quickly. "Tell me, how did you get through the night? Weren't you scared? Did you worry that no one would find you?"

"Nah," answered Roberto. "Our friends helped us."

"Friends? What friends?" asked the reporter.

"Noah," answered Roberto. He winked at the others and they followed one at a time.

"Moses."

"Daniel."

"Joshua."

"Abraham."

"Gideon."

They left the puzzled reporter scratching his head in total confusion. Then the Fairfield Friends headed down the street to Hutch and Ceely's, where family and friends had a huge breakfast waiting for them.

A Fairfield Friends Devotional Adventure

Things to Think About

Why did the Fairfield Friends go into the old factory?

_____

_____

Why couldn't they get out?

_____

_____

Who were their "friends" and how did they "help" the Fairfield Friends?

_____

_____

Read the following passages about each man of faith. What problems faced each one? How did God work out the problem for each?

Noah—Genesis 6–8

_____

_____

Abraham—Genesis 17:1–8, 15–22; 21:1–3.

_____

_____

The Lightning Escape

Moses—Exodus 7:1–7; 12; 14

_____

_____

Joshua—Joshua 6:1–16, 20

_____

_____

Gideon—Judges 6:1–6, 12–16; 7:9–22

_____

_____

Daniel—Daniel 7:17–23

_____

_____

Let's Act It Out!

Memorize Hebrews 11:1.

Act out some of the Bible stories of these men of faith.

Draw a picture of one of them showing faith. For example, draw Noah on the ark, Gideon blowing his trumpet, or Daniel and the lions.

Share a time when you had faith and God worked out the problem or situation. Draw a picture to go with it.

Series for Young Readers*
From Bethany House Publishers

★ ★ ★

THE ADVENTURES OF CALLIE ANN
by Shannon Mason Leppard
Readers will giggle their way through the true-to-life escapades of Callie Ann Davies and her many North Carolina friends.

★ ★ ★

BACKPACK MYSTERIES
by Mary Carpenter Reid
This excitement-filled mystery series follows the mishaps and adventures of Steff and Paulie Larson as they strive to help often-eccentric relatives crack their toughest cases.

★ ★ ★

THE CUL-DE-SAC KIDS
by Beverly Lewis
Each story in this lighthearted series features the hilarious antics and predicaments of nine endearing boys and girls who live on Blossom Hill Lane.

★ ★ ★

RUBY SLIPPERS SCHOOL
by Stacy Towle Morgan
Join the fun as home-schoolers Hope and Annie Brown visit fascinating countries and meet inspiring Christians from around the world!

★ ★ ★

THREE COUSINS DETECTIVE CLUB®
by Elspeth Campbell Murphy
Famous detective cousins Timothy, Titus, and Sarah-Jane learn compelling Scripture-based truths while finding—and solving—intriguing mysteries.

* (ages 7–10)

9611